UNICORNS
OF THE
SECRET STABLE

The Red Key

JOLLY FISH PRESS

Mendota Heights, M

By Whitney Sa

Illustrated by Jomike Tejido

Book design by Sarah Taplin
Illustrations by Jomike Tejido
Illustrations on pages 13, 26, 34 by North Star Editions

Published in the United States by Jolly Fish Press, an imprint of North Star Editions, Inc.

First Edition
First Printing, 2020

This is a work of fiction. Names, characters, places, and incidents are either the product of the author's imagination or are used fictitiously, and any resemblance to actual persons living or dead, business establishments, events, or locales is entirely coincidental.

Library of Congress Cataloging-in-Publication Data (pending)
978-1-63163-396-6 (paperback)
978-1-63163-395-9 (hardcover)

Jolly Fish Press
North Star Editions, Inc.
2297 Waters Drive
Mendota Heights, MN 55120
www.jollyfishpress.com

Printed in the United States of America

TABLE OF CONTENTS

Unicorn Guardians

A long time ago, unicorns and people lived together. When people started hunting the unicorns, two girls decided to help. They used unicorn magic to create a powerful spell. It closed off the Enchanted Realm from the rest of the world. Only the girls' keys could open the Magic Gate.

When the girls grew up, they gave the keys to their daughters. Since then, two young girls have always been the Unicorn Guardians.

CHAPTER 1

Cole's Key

Ruby ducked behind a big rock in the meadow. She waited. A little unicorn face peeked around one side of the rock. Another peeked around the other side.

"You found me!" said Ruby. She laughed as she stood up. She loved playing hide-and-seek with Starsong and Heart's Mirror. The twin foals were getting bigger every day. Their name signs had appeared on their foreheads. These marks showed up after a Guardian named a unicorn.

Iris had named Starsong.

Ruby had named Heart's Mirror.

Ruby glanced up at the sun. It must be nearly time for her to catch the school bus. Her sister, Iris, had already left to wait for it.

Ruby said goodbye to the foals. She hurried across the meadow and walked through the Magic Gate. She lifted the silver key hanging around her neck to lock it.

The key had a fancy wildflower design on its handle. A blue sapphire gem shone in the center. Only Ruby and Iris had keys like it. They were the Unicorn Guardians.

After Ruby went through the gate, the Enchanted Realm disappeared. Something else was disappearing, too— the school bus, as it drove away down the street.

"Wait!" called Ruby. She ran after the bus. But it was too late.

Ruby rode her bike to school. Class had started by the time she got there. It was show-and-tell day. She tiptoed to her seat.

Cole stood at the front of the classroom. He was a new student. He was also her neighbor. His family had moved into the house across the street from Ruby's. He was wearing a *Dragon Rider* video game T-shirt.

"I brought something that my grandpa gave me," said Cole. He opened his hand and showed it to the class.

Ruby couldn't believe what she saw. It was a key. It looked just like her key to the Enchanted Realm.

But Cole's key was different in some ways. It was gold instead of silver. It had flames engraved on it instead of wildflowers. And it had a fiery red gem instead of a blue one.

Ruby raised her hand. "What does your key open?" she asked.

"I don't know," said Cole. "My grandpa died last year. He wanted me to have this. But he didn't say what it was for."

Ruby found Cole at recess. She showed him her silver key. But she had to say she didn't know what it opened. She had to keep the Enchanted Realm a secret.

But she wondered, *How did Cole's grandpa get the key? Had he been a Unicorn Guardian?*

What if Cole was a Guardian too?

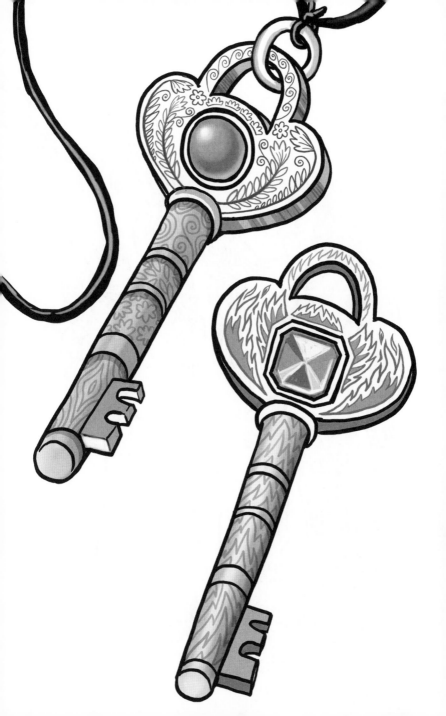

CHAPTER 2

Dragon Attack!

After school, Ruby found Iris with the unicorns. She was braiding tiny bluebells into Heartsong's mane. Heartsong's twins were napping nearby.

Ruby started to tell Iris about Cole's key. But she stopped. She smelled smoke in the air.

Iris sniffed. "What's that?" she asked. "I hope there isn't a fire in the Fairy Forest!"

Ruby heard a distant roaring sound.

She saw something flying in the distance.

It was coming from the Fire Mountains,

beyond the forest. It looked like a bird.

But it was much bigger.

The creature was flying fast toward them. But it wasn't a bird. It was a dragon!

"Dragon attack!" yelled Ruby.

The unicorns saw the dragon too. They started galloping toward the Fairy Forest. The thick trees would shelter them.

The twin foals scrambled to their feet.

They ran next to their mother on spindly legs.

The dragon flew low over the meadow. It breathed fire from its mouth. The flames scorched the grass and flowers.

Iris and Ruby ran beside the unicorns. They helped lead them into the safety of the woods. When the girls reached the trees, they looked back.

Starsong had fallen behind. The dragon stretched out its claws and scooped her up.

"No!" cried Iris.

Ruby watched in horror as the dragon flew away. It carried Starsong back toward the Fire Mountains.

Heartsong whinnied for her foal. But Starsong was already gone.

CHAPTER 3

The Fire Mountains

"I can't believe Starsong is gone," whispered Ruby. Her eyes filled with tears.

Heartsong reared up on her hind legs.

She looked like she wanted to fly into the air after Starsong. But without wings, she couldn't fly.

"I think we can get her back," said Iris. Her face was pale, and her voice was shaky. "I read about dragons in the *Book of Unicorns*."

The *Book of Unicorns* was filled with advice from earlier Guardians. Iris had read more of it than Ruby.

"Dragons only feast once a month," said Iris. "And only under the light of the full moon. If we can find Starsong before then, we can save her."

Ruby pictured how the moon had looked last night. It had been almost full. Just a tiny sliver was missing.

"I think the next full moon is tonight," she said.

Iris nodded. "We have to go now. And we'll have to ride on unicorns. The Fire Mountains are too far for us to walk."

"Won't the unicorns be afraid?" asked Ruby.

"Unicorns can be fierce in battle when they need to be," said Iris.

That didn't make Ruby feel much better. How could they win a battle with a dragon? It seemed hopeless.

Starfire walked over to Ruby. He was the foals' father. He wanted to help get Starsong back. But Ruby could see that he was limping. He must have tripped running into the woods.

"I'm sorry," said Ruby, patting his neck. "You need to rest now."

Ruby couldn't ride Heartsong either. She needed to stay with Heart's Mirror.

Ruby walked up to Tempest. He was the biggest and wildest of the unicorns. If any unicorn could face a dragon, it was him. "We need your help," she said.

Tempest tossed his head. Then he bowed down on one knee. He was giving her permission to ride him.

Iris went up to another unicorn stallion, Cloud Shadow. But he shied away from her. He didn't want to go to the Fire Mountains.

Another unicorn came up to Iris and bowed. It was Moonlight Melody.

She was Starsong and Heart's Mirror's older sister. She was still young, but she was one of the fastest unicorns.

The girls mounted their unicorns.

"Who is that?" asked Iris.

Ruby turned and saw someone coming toward them across the meadow. It was Cole!

"How did you get here?" asked Ruby.

"I looked out my bedroom window earlier," said Cole. "I saw you go into the pasture behind the barn. Then you disappeared. I wanted to follow you, but the gate was locked. So I opened it with my key."

He held up the gold key with the red jewel on the handle.

"What is this place?" he asked. "Are these *unicorns*?" He reached out to touch Tempest's long dark mane.

"Yes. Unicorns are real," Ruby said impatiently. She didn't have time to explain everything. "So are dragons," she said. "A dragon just took one of the unicorns. We have to rescue her."

Cole's eyes widened. "Wow," he said. "Can I come with you? I've beaten every level of *Dragon Rider*. Maybe I can help."

Ruby and Iris looked at each other. A

video game was not the same as real life.

Iris shook her head.

"Only the Guardians are allowed in the Enchanted Realm," said Ruby.

"Anyway, it could be dangerous," added Iris.

"I'm not afraid," said Cole. "And I'm not leaving!"

Tempest pawed at the ground. Moonlight Melody tossed her head. They wanted to go. There was no time to waste.

"Okay," said Ruby. She reached down to help Cole onto Tempest's back. He sat behind her.

"Where are we going?" he asked.

Ruby pointed toward the mountains in the distance. One of the peaks glowed red, like embers from a fire.

"There," she said.

CHAPTER 4

A New Guardian

It took over an hour to reach the Fire Mountains. First, they rode through the Fairy Forest. Then they climbed up steep, slippery rocks. The air got hotter. The rocks began to glow.

"Starsong!" cried Ruby.

The unicorn was in a pen made from a circle of huge rocks. The dragon perched on one of them.

The dragon saw the kids. It spread its leathery wings. Then it swooped down and landed in front of them.

Tempest reared up on his hind legs. Ruby clung to his mane. But Cole fell off.

His key fell out of his pocket. It bounced and landed on the ground in front of the dragon.

The dragon stopped. It stared at the key. The gem was the same color as the dragon's bright-red eyes.

Cole got up slowly. He picked up his key.

The dragon took a step closer. It spread its huge wings. Smoke puffed from its nostrils.

Cole held up the key. "Do you want this?" he asked the dragon. "I'll give it to you if you don't hurt us."

Then the dragon did something that none of them expected. It lowered its long neck. It rested its head in front of Cole.

"Is . . . is it bowing?" Cole asked.

"Yes," said Iris. Her voice was filled with wonder. "Just like the unicorns bow to let us ride them."

"Cole, you are a Guardian!" said Ruby.

"But not of unicorns."

Cole faced the dragon. He stared for a long moment, unsure of what to do.

The dragon flared out its wings. They were so big they blocked out the sun.

Ruby could see Cole shaking with fear. But he stood as tall as he could.

"I am the Dragon Guardian," he said. "I know you must eat, but you may not eat unicorns. I forbid them from being hunted."

Ruby thought he sounded like a prince from a fairy tale. But would the dragon listen?

At first, the dragon looked angry. It lifted its head and breathed a jet of fire.

But then it backed away from the stone pen.

Ruby and Iris rode forward. With Tempest's and Moonlight Melody's help, they tried to push away one of the big stones. But it was too heavy.

"Dragon," said Cole, "release this unicorn."

The dragon swooped into the air.

It grabbed Starsong in its claws. She

whinnied with fear.

The dragon put Starsong down in front of Ruby and Iris. The girls rushed to comfort the foal.

Then the dragon landed beside Cole. It lowered its huge head. Cole reached out and stroked its scales. The dragon made a noise that was almost like purring.

"We should go," said Ruby. "Starsong needs to get back to her mother."

"You go on," said Cole. His eyes were on the dragon. "There is something else I want to do here."

Ruby and Iris rode back down the mountain. Starsong trotted between them. Tempest and Midnight Melody slowed their steps so she could keep up.

The group passed through the Fairy Forest. The sun was low in the sky now. Ruby hoped they would make it home before nighttime.

The Red Key

Finally, they reached the meadow. Starsong cantered ahead. Heartsong came out of the forest to meet her. She nuzzled Starsong all over, making sure she was okay.

A shadow fell over them. Ruby looked up. Iris gasped. The dragon was back! Had it hurt Cole? Had it come to steal more unicorns?

Ruby noticed the rider on the dragon's back. Cole waved to her. Ruby waved back.

The dragon turned and swooped away. Soon, it was just a tiny shape flying toward the setting sun.

THINK ABOUT IT

 Think about what you would do if you had a key and did not know what it opened.

 Ruby and Iris take care of the unicorns. What chores do you do at home?

 Imagine you had your own unicorn. Tell a friend what you would name it and what it would look like.

ABOUT THE AUTHOR

Whitney Sanderson grew up riding horses as a member of a 4-H club and competing in local jumping and dressage shows. She has written several books in the Horse Diaries chapter book series. She is also the author of *Horse Rescue: Treasure*, based on her time volunteering at an equine rescue farm. She lives in Massachusetts.

ABOUT THE ILLUSTRATOR

Jomike Tejido is an author and illustrator of the picture book *There Was an Old Woman Who Lived in a Book*. He also illustrated the Pet Charms and My Magical Friends leveled reader series. He has fond memories of horseback riding as a kid and has always loved drawing magical creatures. Jomike lives in Manila with his wife, two daughters, and a chow chow named Oso.

RETURN TO MAGIC MOON STABLE

Book 1

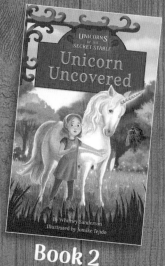

Book 2

Book 3

Book 4

AVAILABLE NOW